ONE GIRL'S VOICE

How Lucy Stone Helped Change the Law of the Land

Written by Vivian Kirkfield   Illustrated by Rebecca Gibbon

CALKINS CREEK

AN IMPRINT OF ASTRA BOOKS FOR YOUNG READERS

New York

Lucy's ideas, thoughts, and opinions bubbled up,
ready to spill out. But in 1830, in Massachusetts
and across the United States, the law said the
voices of girls and women didn't count.

At home, Lucy simmered when her mother submitted
to her husband's rule.

"There was only one will in our Home and it was my FATHER'S."

At school, Lucy stewed when the teacher called on the boys even though *her* hand shot up first.

And at church, Lucy steamed when the minister warned against letting women speak in public. Perched on the edge of her seat, Lucy poked her cousin each time she heard an unjust word of the sermon.

Right then and there, Lucy made up her mind that when she grew up, if she had anything to say, she would say it!

Lucy set out to prove her voice mattered. But even though she added sums faster and memorized verses better than her brothers, her father refused to buy her schoolbooks. Lucy collected nuts and berries to sell for book money.

And when her father said she already had enough education for a female, Lucy resolved to earn her *own* money to pay for college tuition.

"I went to the woods, with my bare little toes, and gathered chestnuts and sold them for money enough to buy the book. I felt a prouder sense of triumph than I have ever known since."

She sewed shoes,

and tutored schoolchildren.

sold jam,

She saved her pennies, nickels, and dimes until she had enough.

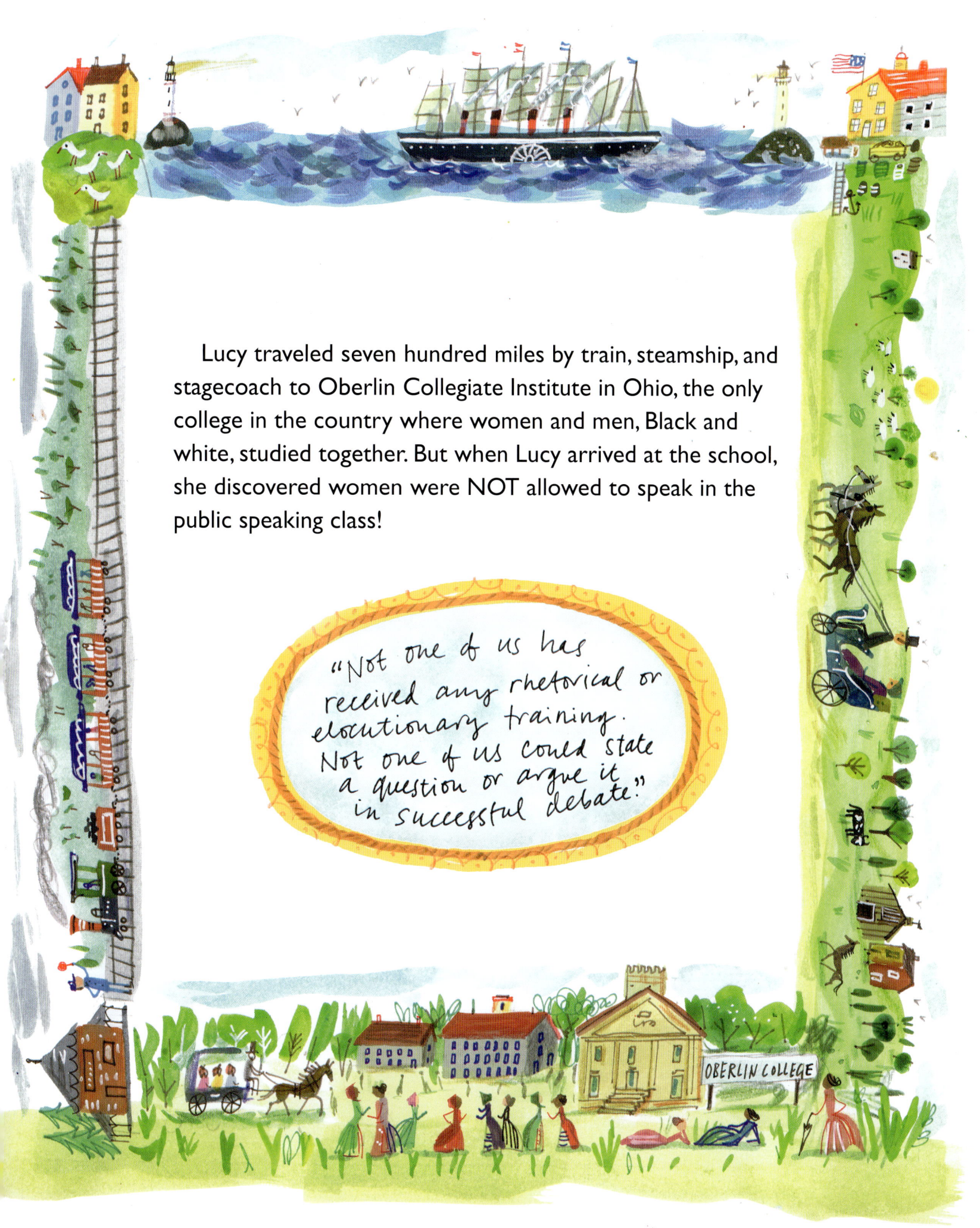

Lucy traveled seven hundred miles by train, steamship, and stagecoach to Oberlin Collegiate Institute in Ohio, the only college in the country where women and men, Black and white, studied together. But when Lucy arrived at the school, she discovered women were NOT allowed to speak in the public speaking class!

"Not one of us has received any rhetorical or elocutionary training. Not one of us could state a question or argue it in successful debate."

Lucy cooked up a plan,
quietly spread the word to a few female friends,
and snuck off with them to a cabin in the woods.

While some of the women kept watch outside, the other members of this secret debating club sharpened their speeches, polished their arguments, and countered each challenge. Now how could they put their skills to the test?

Lucy begged a favor of her professor. Would he allow the women to speak in the classroom? He'd be breaking the rules. But Lucy had already mastered the skill of persuasive argument. She won him over!

One afternoon, the members of the secret club got their chance. Words flew back and forth as the young women challenged each other's point of view. Classmates cheered! But when the school administration found out, they banned all future debates by women. Lucy swallowed her words, but before long, she found another way to make her voice heard.

"ONLY LET FEMALES BE EDUCATED IN THE SAME MANNER AND WITH THE SAME ADVANTAGES THAT MALES HAVE, AND, AS EVERYTHING IN NATURE SEEKS ITS OWN LEVEL, I WOULD RISK THAT WE WOULD FIND OUT OUR 'APPROPRIATE SPHERE.'"

Lucy scrubbed floors, swept stairs, and taught classes to pay for her room and meals at the college. When she learned that female students received only half as much pay as males even though they did the same work, her anger boiled over.

She wrote a letter of complaint to the school board, but Lucy's arguments on paper were not enough. Standing firm, Lucy refused to teach any more classes until she received equal pay.

Week after week, Lucy waited.

Finally, school officials announced their decision. All students who worked at Oberlin would receive the same pay for the same work. Lucy celebrated! And before long, she secured another opportunity to make her voice heard.

Miss Lucy Stone
Oberlin College
Oberlin, Ohio

Her heart raced and her hands shook as she held an invitation to compose a speech for the graduation ceremony. She closed her eyes and saw herself at the podium, speaking. Triumphant, Lucy rejoiced . . .

. . . until school officials informed her that only a male student would be allowed to read the speech.

"I certainly shall not write if I cannot read for myself," Lucy wrote to her parents.

On graduation day, Lucy did not speak at the podium. But she *did* speak with one of the guests, William Lloyd Garrison, head of the New England Anti-Slavery Society, an organization working to put an end to slavery. "I expect to plead not for the slave only, but for suffering humanity everywhere," Lucy said. "Especially do I mean to labor for the elevation of my sex." Garrison recognized the power of her words and the passion in her voice. And he soon hired Lucy to work for the society.

"I went from City to City and from State to State, everywhere carrying the good gospel of equal rights for women, seeking to create that wholesome discontent among women which would make them resent their unequal condition, and wish to escape from it."

Lucy's voice rang out at rallies in small town halls and echoed in big city auditoriums. Some called her the Silver Bell, the Morning Star, and the Orator because her words inspired thousands who attended her lectures. But speaking out for human rights was dangerous, especially for a woman who wasn't supposed to be speaking at all.

When mobs gathered to protest, Lucy spoke louder.

When men hurled books and rotten vegetables, Lucy stood taller.

And when a hose doused her with ice-cold water, Lucy kept speaking.

Nothing could put out the fire in her heart.

Throughout her marriage to Henry Blackwell, Lucy continued her speaking tours. Only the birth of her daughter spurred her to step back from them. But caring for young Alice reminded Lucy of the plight of women in America. She knew that change would come only if people spoke out and demanded it.

 She traveled by horse,

 by train,

 and by foot.

 She braved snowstorms,

blistering heat,

and driving rain.

She slept in beds with dirty sheets—

when there were sheets.

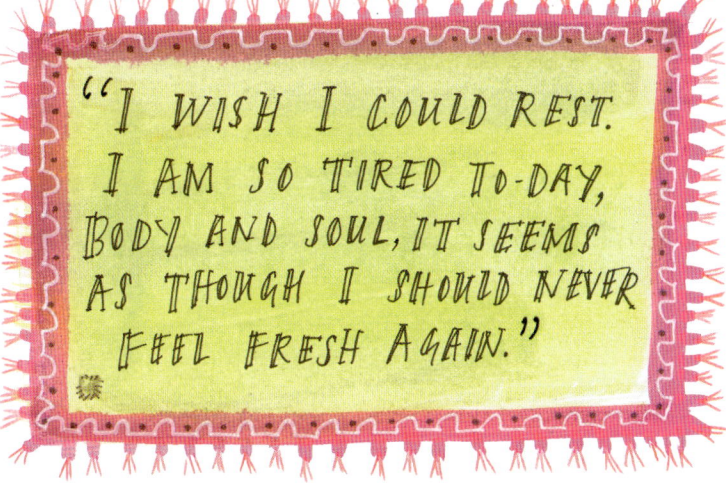

"I WISH I COULD REST. I AM SO TIRED TO-DAY, BODY AND SOUL, IT SEEMS AS THOUGH I SHOULD NEVER FEEL FRESH AGAIN."

And sometimes she shared a room with people she did not even know.

Step by step, Lucy fought for change. She helped rally
men and women to sign petitions, and Congress passed the
Thirteenth Amendment, which abolished slavery. She spoke
before the New Jersey legislature, and soon a law gave
married women property rights. And when Lucy was
sixty-five years old, Oberlin College invited her to return
for their fiftieth anniversary.

"And what is the result of this example of Oberlin of fifty years of co-education?... All around behold more than half the colleges of the land wide open to women."

No longer barred from speaking, Lucy Stone stood on the podium and shared her ideas, thoughts, and opinions . . .

... because one girl's voice helped change the law of the land so that all voices *could* be heard.

"I HAVE DONE WHAT I WANTED TO DO. I HAVE HELPED THE WOMEN."

When Lucy Stone graduated from Oberlin College in 1847,
she became the first Massachusetts woman to earn a
four-year university degree.

AUTHOR'S NOTE

I got married in 1967, more than one hundred years after Lucy Stone spoke up for the rights of women, but there were still many changes that needed to be made. With a college degree and a license to teach elementary school, I still could not obtain a credit card in my name—my husband was required to cosign. It wasn't until the Equal Credit Opportunity Act of 1974 that women in America could apply for credit cards and mortgages on their own. And we are still fighting the battle that Lucy Stone dedicated her life to—gender equality in employment, a place on the political platform, and equal rights for all. But, thanks to the determination, sacrifice, and perseverance of Lucy and others, slavery was abolished, and women in America can vote, speak in public, and are equal partners in their families.

A flyer advertising a meeting where Lucy Stone and her husband, Henry Blackwell, would be speaking in support of the Equal Rights Movement.

H. B. BLACKWELL
AND
LUCY STONE!

These uncompromising friends of Freedom and untiring advocates of Human Rights propose to meet the citizens of Vineland at

PLUM ST. HALL,

This,
Tuesday Evening, Dec. 4,
AT 7:30,
TO PRESENT THE

Equal Rights Movement

And organize a Club.

Let no one fail to come and see and hear these pioneer Reformers, who have devoted their lives to the cause of Liberty and now in the vigor of manhood and womanhood come amongst us to ask our help to obtain for all mankind Human Rights.

It is to be regretted that they can be with us but ONE night.

SEATS FREE.

TIMELINE OF LUCY STONE AND THE FIGHT FOR WOMEN'S RIGHTS AND EQUALITY FOR ALL

August 13, 1818: Lucy Stone is born in West Brookfield, Massachusetts.

1847: Lucy Stone becomes first woman from Massachusetts to graduate with a BA degree.

1848: Declaration of Sentiments, a plea for the end of discrimination against women.

1850: Lucy Stone helps organize the first National Women's Rights Convention.

1863: Emancipation Proclamation abolishes slavery in the Southern states.

1865: The Thirteenth Amendment abolishes slavery in all states.

1866: Lucy Stone, Elizabeth Cady Stanton, and Susan B. Anthony form the American Equal Rights Association (AERA), dedicated to suffrage for all regardless of gender or race.

1869: Wyoming passes America's first women's suffrage law.

1870: The Fifteenth Amendment gives Black men the right to vote, but many are prevented from doing so, especially in southern states.

1872: Susan B. Anthony is arrested for voting in a presidential election.

1890: National Woman Suffrage Association (NWSA) and American Woman Suffrage Association (AWSA) merge to secure suffrage at the state level.

1916: Jeannette Rankin (Montana), first woman elected to the US House of Representatives.

1919: The Senate passes the Nineteenth Amendment—woman suffrage.

1920: American women win full voting rights.

1932: Hattie Wyatt Caraway, first woman elected to the US Senate.

1933: Frances Perkins, first female cabinet member, appointed secretary of labor.

1963: Equal Pay Act prohibits gender-based wage discrimination.

1964: Title VII of the Civil Rights Act bans employment discrimination.

An 1853 *Illustrated News* engraving of Lucy Stone wearing the "Bloomer" costume for her lecture in New York City.

1972: Title IX of the Education Amendments protects against discrimination in any program receiving federal financial assistance.

1981: Sandra Day O'Connor, first woman to serve on the US Supreme Court.

1984: Geraldine Ferraro, first woman vice president nominee by a major party.

1993: Janet Reno, first female attorney general of the United States.

1997: Madeleine Albright, first female US Secretary of State.

2007: US Rep. Nancy Pelosi, first female Speaker of the House.

2013: The US military removes a ban against women serving in combat positions.

2016: Hillary Clinton, first woman presidential nominee from a major political party.

2021: Kamala Harris, first woman, first Black, and first South Asian vice president.

In 1857, Lucy Stone gave birth to a daughter. When Alice grew up, she continued her mother's work and united with the daughter of Elizabeth Cady Stanton to advocate for women's suffrage.

FUN FACTS

By the time Lucy was a third-year student at Oberlin, her father had grown to admire her courage, and he respected her incredible work ethic. She wrote a letter to the family, detailing how she rose at 5:00 a.m. and did not get to bed until 2:00 or 3:00 a.m. because in addition to her studies, she worked at several jobs for only a few cents an hour in order to pay for her room and board at the college. Her father answered her on January 11, 1845: "There will be no trouble about money, you can have what you need, without studying nights or working for eight cents an hour."

● Elizabeth Cady Stanton wrote, "Lucy Stone was the first speaker who really stirred the nation's heart on the subject of woman's wrongs."

● Inspired to join the women's rights movement after reading a newspaper article about Lucy's speech at the Worcester convention, Susan B. Anthony said, "I made up my mind then that no one would make a relict [widow] out of me."

● Lucy founded the *Woman's Journal* in 1870, which became the most popular woman's newspaper of the time and was a platform for many women to share their views.

● Lucy defied gender norms when she and her husband-to-be wrote marriage vows to reflect their egalitarian beliefs, taking out the word "obey."

● Women who retained their own name after marriage were called Lucy Stoners. Although these days many women choose to take their husband's surname after marriage, those that don't are not denied legal rights, as women were in Lucy's time.

● Lucy thought it unfair that women were required to pay taxes, even though they could not hold office, own property, or vote. When her tax bill came due, Lucy mailed the unpaid bill with a letter: "Sir: Enclosed I return my tax bill, without paying it. My reason for doing so, is, that women suffer taxation, and yet have no representation, which is not only unjust to one half of the adult population, but is contrary to our theory of government." Sadly, the tax department did not agree with Lucy. They confiscated her furniture and auctioned off everything to pay the taxes. Fortunately, kind neighbors bought the items and returned them to Lucy.

This sculpture of Lucy Stone is part of the Boston Women's Memorial and was created by artist Meredith Bergmann.

BIBLIOGRAPHY

All quotations used in the book can be found in the following sources marked with an asterisk (*).

*Adams, J., Blackwell, A. S., Fawcett, M. G., Harper, I. H., Parkhurst, E., Shaw, A. H. & Stanton, E. C. *Women of the Suffrage Movement: Memoirs & Biographies of the Most Influential Suffragettes.* Prague: Madison & Adams Press, 2018.

Blackwell, Henry, and Lucy Stone. *Marriage Protest.* May 1, 1855; reprinted 1897. Blackwell Family Papers, Manuscript Division, Library of Congress (020.00.00).

Cambo, Carol. "Lucy Stone Lost and Found." *Oberlin Alumni Magazine* 99, no. 4 (Spring 2004).

Kerr, Andrea Moore. *Lucy Stone: Speaking Out for Equality.* New Brunswick: Rutgers University Press, 1992.

McMillen, Sally G. *Lucy Stone: An Unapologetic Life.* New York: Oxford University Press, 2015.

Michals, Debra, ed. "Lucy Stone." National Women's History Museum. womenshistory.org/education-resources/biographies/lucy-stone.

Million, Joelle. *Woman's Voice, Woman's Place: Lucy Stone and the Birth of the Woman's Rights Movement.* Westport, CT: Prager Publishers, 2003.

Rice, Elinor. *Those Extraordinary Blackwells.* New York: Harcourt, Brace & World, Inc., 1967.

Schlesinger Library on the History of Women in America. *Lucy Stone Papers in the Woman's Rights Collection. Suffrage documents, 1866–1915.* WRC, folder 1053. Schlesinger Library, Radcliffe Institute, Harvard University, Cambridge, MA. nrs.harvard.edu/urn-3:RAD.SCHL:37693958.

*Stone, Lucy. "The Progress of Fifty Years." World's Columbian Exposition speech, 1898.

*———. "Disappointment Is the Lot of Women." Reprinted in *History of Woman Suffrage* 1, edited by Elizabeth Cady Stanton. New York: Fowler and Wells, 1922, 165–67.

*———. "Oberlin and Woman." Speech at Oberlin College Fiftieth Anniversary, June 1887. oberlin.edu/external/EOG/Booklets/Jubilee%20Notes%20folder/JubileeNotes2.html#JubileeWomen.

Wagner, Sally, ed. *The Women's Suffrage Movement.* New York: Penguin Random House, 2019.

Waxman, Olivia B. "'Lucy Stone, If You Please': The Unsung Suffragist Who Fought for Women to Keep Their Maiden Names." *Time,* March 7, 2019. time.com/5537834/lucy-stone-maiden-names-womens-history.

Woman's Rights Convention, Lucy Stone, National American Woman Suffrage Association Collection, and Susan B. Anthony Collection. *The proceedings of the Woman's Rights Convention, held at Worcester, October 23d & 24th.* Boston: Prentiss & Sawyer, 1851. Pdf. loc.gov/item/93838286/.

ACKNOWLEDGMENTS

It definitely takes a village to make a book. Thank you to my critique buddies, especially Beth Anderson, Tina Cho, Carrie Finison, Hannah Holt, Alayne Kay Christian, Diane Tulloch, and Hanh Bui who are always ready at a moment's notice to provide feedback. Thank you to my agent, Essie White, who champions all of my stories and to Calkins Creek's editorial director Carolyn Yoder and associate editor Thalia Leaf who saw promise in the manuscript and wouldn't let me give up until I got it right. And thank you to Judith Kalaora, Lucy Stone historical interpreter and artistic director of History At Play, LLC, whose portrayal of Lucy Stone inspired me to write this story. —VK

To my granddaughters, Emily and Sophie. Because of women like Lucy Stone, we have the right to make our voices heard. I hope we use it to help those whose rights are threatened and whose voices are silenced. —VK

For Ray Chan —RG

Picture Credits

Library of Congress: LC-USZ6-2055: 34, mss12880, box 85, reel 68: 35, 2005677274: 37; Kansas Historical Society: 36; Lucy Stone, Boston Women's Memorial, Meredith Bergmann 2003, photo by Meredith Bergmann: 38.

Calkins Creek
An imprint of Astra Books for Young Readers,
a division of Astra Publishing House
astrapublishinghouse.com
Printed in China

ISBN: 978-1-6626-8045-8 (hc)
ISBN: 978-1-6626-8046-5 (eBook)
Library of Congress Control Number: 2024932222

First edition

10 9 8 7 6 5 4 3 2 1

Design by Barbara Grzeslo
The text is set in Gill Sans Std.
The illustrations are painted in acrylic ink and colored pencil.